Silent Cry

Aayush Maatrishya

Maatrishya

Copyright © 2024 Aayush Maatrishya

All rights reserved.

Cover design by: Aayush Maatrishya

For inquiries or permissions requests, please contact:
maatrishya@gmail.com

To all the silent souls who long to be heard

and understood.

"There is no greater agony than bearing an untold story inside you."

– Maya Angelou

Contents

Introduction

This is a collection of poems written for someone who has a lot to say, but doesn't know how to say it.

Someone who hides their true feelings behind a mask of strength and happiness, but inside they are hurting and broken.

Someone who feels alone and misunderstood, and fears being judged or rejected if they open up. These poems are their way of expressing their inner turmoil, their silent struggles, and their hidden desires.

These poems are also a deep exploration of what it means to be human, to face the challenges and contradictions of life, and to seek connection and acceptance. Each poem tells a story of a different aspect of their journey, revealing their emotions, thoughts, and experiences.

These poems are like a musical composition, where each note is a word, each line is a melody, and each stanza is a harmony. Together, they create a beautiful and powerful symphony of silent cries that speaks to the heart and soul of the reader.

These poems are not just about one person; they are about all of us. They reflect the complexity and diversity of our minds and hearts, and the common themes and issues that we all face. They invite us to think deeply about ourselves and others, and to empathize with the pain, longing, and vulnerability that we all share.

These poems are a celebration of our humanity, and a reminder that we are not alone in our quest for meaning and understanding in this vast and mysterious world.

****

With the blessing of "Lord Ganesha"

1st Prose

I

I hide my pain behind a smile,

But inside I'm dying all the while,

No one hears my silent scream,

No one knows my broken dream.

II

I wish I could let it all out,

But I'm afraid of the doubt,

That would fill their eyes,

If they heard my silent cries.

III

I pretend to be strong and brave,

But I feel like a lonely slave,

To the sorrow that consumes my soul,

To the darkness that takes its toll.

IV

I long for someone to understand,

To hold me close and take my hand,

To heal my wounds and ease my fears,

To wipe away my bitter tears.

V

But I know it's just a fantasy,

A wish that will never be,

So I keep on hiding my pain behind a smile,

And I keep on dying inside all the while.

****

2nd Prose

VI

The world is loud, but I am quiet,

I have no voice, I can't deny it,

I want to speak, but words won't come,

I feel like, I'm insane.

VII

I try to laugh, but tears fall down,

I try to stand, but I fall to the ground,

I try to live, but I want to die,

The only sound I make is a silent cry.

VIII

I see the joy in others' faces,

I hear the cheers in crowded places,

I smell the flowers in the spring,

I taste the sweetness life can bring.

IX

But I can't touch any of it,

I can't feel any of it,

I'm trapped in a shell of despair,

I'm lost in a world of nowhere.

X

I wish I could break free from this,

I wish I could find some bliss,

But I know it's just a lie,

The only truth I have is a silent cry.

****

3rd Prose

XI

You left me alone, without a goodbye,

You took away my love, you made me cry

But I can't show my feelings,

I have to be strong,

I can't let them see, what you did wrong

XII

So I keep it inside, I lock it away,

I pretend like I'm okay, on every day

But at night, when I'm alone, I can't lie,

I break down and sob, I let out a silent cry

XIII

You were my everything, my reason to live,

You gave me so much; you had so much to give

But you betrayed me, you broke my heart,

You tore me apart, you left a scar

XIV

Now I'm barren, I'm vacant, I'm frozen,

I have no one to cherish, no one to embrace

I'm trapped in a horror, I can't escape,

I'm sinking in misery, I can't rise up

XV

But I have to hide it, I have to smile,

I have to act like I'm fine, I have to lie

But deep inside, I'm still hurting, I still cry,

The only sound I make is a silent cry

****

4th Prose

XVI

I'm trapped in a cage, made of fear and shame,

I'm hurt by the words, of hate and blame

I can't escape; even I can't fight back,

I can't defend, even I can't attack

XVII

I'm empty, I'm numb,

I have no one to adore, no one to hug

I'm stuck in a terror, I can't break free,

I'm submerged in anguish, I can't lay

I have no hope, I have no way

XVIII

I can only suffer, I can only sigh,

I can only whimper, I can only cry

A silent cry, that no one hears,

A silent cry, that drowns in tears

IX

Of what I've lost, the memories haunt me

Of what I've cost, the regrets torment me

I can't forget, nor can I forgive

I can't move on, nor can I live

XX

I am broken, and I am shattered

I am damaged, and I am wounded

I am scarred, and I am ravaged

I have no faith, I have no trust,

I have no love, I have no lust

XXI

I can only bleed, I can only ache,

I can only mourn, I can only break

A silent cry, that no one feels,

A silent cry, that never heals

****

5th Prose

XXII

I have a secret, that I can't share,

I have a burden, which I can't bear

I have a wound, that I can't heal,

I have a pain, which I can't feel

XXIII

I have a story, that I can't tell,

I have a hell, which I can't quell

I have a silence, that I can't break,

I have a cry, which I can't make

A silent cry, that burns my soul,

A silent cry, which takes its toll

XXIV

The fear, the shame, I can't face or erase

The dread, the stain, I can't chase or replace

I have a guilt, that I can't forgive,

I have a grief that I can't live

XXV

I have a dream, that I can't pursue,

I have a love that I can't renew

I have a faith, that I can't restore,

I have a hope that I can't explore

XXVI

I have a life, that I can't enjoy,

I have a heart that I can't employ

A silent cry, that shatters my core,

A silent cry, that asks for more

****

6th Prose

XXVII

I have a smile, that I can't share,

I have a joy that I can't spare

I have a love, that I can't show,

I have a soul that I can't grow

XXVIII

I have a mask, that I can't remove,

I have a role that I can't improve

I have a lie, that I can't confess,

I have a pain that I can't express

XXIX

A silent cry, that fills my chest,

A silent cry that steals my rest

XXX

I have a secret, that I can't reveal,

I have a wound that I can't heal

I have a fear, that I can't face,

I have a shame that I can't erase

XXXI

I have a foe that I can't adjust

I have a family, that I can't please,

I have a world that I can't appease

XXXII

A silent cry, that clouds my sight,

A silent cry that dims my light

****

7th Prose

XXXIII

I have a past, that I can't forget,

I have a future that I can't predict

I have a present, that I can't enjoy,

I have a life that I can't employ

XXXIV

I have a mistake, that I can't undo,

I have a regret that I can't subdue

I have a loss, that I can't recover,

I have a wound that I can't cover

XXXV

A silent cry, that haunts my mind,

A silent cry that leaves me behind

XXXVI

I have a hope, that I can't fulfill,

I have a faith that I can't instill

I have a grace, that I can't earn,

I have a sin, that I can't burn

XXXVII

I have a dream, that I can't achieve,

I have a goal, that I can't conceive

I have a talent, that I can't use,

I have a gift that I can't refuse

XXXVIII

A silent cry, that shatters my core,

A silent cry, that asks for more

****

8th Prose

XXXIX

I have a friend, that I can't trust,

I have a foe that I can't adjust

I have a family, that I can't please,

I have a world that I can't appease

XL

I have a dream, that I can't achieve,

I have a goal that I can't conceive

I have a talent, that I can't use,

I have a gift that I can't refuse

XLI

A silent cry, that breaks my will,

A silent cry, that keeps me still

XLII

I have a love, that I can't express,

I have a heart that I can't impress

I have a soul, that I can't connect,

I have a spirit that I can't protect

XLIII

I have a pain, that I can't heal,

I have a wound, that can't be seal

I have a loss, that I can't mourn,

I have a life, that I can't adorn

XLIV

A silent cry, that tears me apart,

A silent cry, that pierces my heart

****

9th Prose

XLV

I have a heart, that I can't heal,

I have a wound that I can't seal

I have a love, that I can't keep,

I have a loss that I can't weep

XLVI

I have a hope, that I can't fulfill,

I have a faith that I can't instill

I have a grace, that I can't earn,

I have a sin that I can't burn

XLVII

A silent cry, that stains my soul,

A silent cry that takes its toll

XLVIII

I have a memory, that I can't erase,

I have a face that I can't replace

I have a bond, that I can't mend,

I have a friend that I can't defend

XLIX

I have a guilt, that I can't release,

I have a peace that I can't increase

I have a pain, that I can't endure,

I have a cure that I can't procure

L

A silent cry, that fills my eyes,

A silent cry, that never dies

****

10th Prose

LI

I have a voice, that I can't raise,

I have a word that I can't praise

I have a song, that I can't sing,

I have a melody that I can't ring

LII

I have a story, that I can't write,

I have a vision that I can't sight

I have a poem, that I can't create,

I have a rhyme that I can't relate

LIII

A silent cry, that mutes my art,

A silent cry that chokes my heart

LIV

I have a passion, that I can't ignite,

I have a fire that I can't light

I have a color, that I can't paint,

I have a beauty that I can't taint

LV

I have a message, that I can't convey,

I have a meaning that I can't portray

I have a wisdom, that I can't impart,

I have a truth that I can't start

LVI

A silent cry, that dims my spark,

A silent cry that leaves me dark

LVII

With all lost terms and a voice about to die,

I finally am left, screaming a silent cry……

****

Maatrishya Uvach

Mummy Kehti Hai Humari Chapter 16 verse 12: *"People hide behind fake smiles and pretty pictures."*

I think it is a complex and subjective topic, so better to leave this.

Coming back to the poems, I wrote them over the years, going through ups and downs, joys and sorrows, successes and failures. They are the outcomes of my observations, reflections, and expressions.

I wrote these poems for you, to reach out, communicate, and connect to those "Silent Souls" who need to be heard and understood.

We have to understand this: People may seem confident but struggle with anxiety. They may appear healthy but suffer from pain. They may smile but hide their misery. They may look beautiful but feel insecure. Therefore, we should be kind, as everyone is fighting a battle and we know nothing about it.

I hope you found something in them that touched you, moved you, or challenged you or inspired you.

Aayush Maatrishya

****

Epilogue

These poems are the silent cries of a soul. They are the expressions of an inner turmoil, hidden desires, and unspoken emotions. They are the reflections of a human experience, challenges and contradictions, and hopes and dreams. They are the connections with fellow travelers, empathizers and supporters, and friends and lovers.

These poems are a gift to you, dear reader. They are an invitation to you to enter a world, to share feelings, and to understand thoughts. They are a request to you to listen to a voice, to appreciate a perspective, and to respect choices. They are a hope for you to find meaning, inspiration, and joy in words.

These poems are a legacy, a contribution to the world. They are a way of leaving a mark, of making a difference, and of creating a change. They are a way of saying that someone was here, that someone mattered, and that someone loved.

****

Afterword

Meet you in "If this is the end......."

Aayush Maatrishya

Acknowledgement

"Silent Cry"

I would like to express my heartfelt gratitude to everyone who contributed to the creation of the story "Silent Cry" This story would not have been possible without the support, inspiration, and dedication of many individuals.

First and foremost, I want to thank the *'Maate.'*

I extend my sincere appreciation to my family for their unwavering encouragement and belief in my writing. Your constant support has been my driving force.

To the readers of my work, your enthusiasm and passion for storytelling are my greatest motivation. Thank you for joining in this Silent Journey.

Last but not least, I want to acknowledge the power of storytelling itself. It is a universal language that connects us all, and

I am grateful to be a part of this beautiful tradition.

Very-very thank you the *'Uncommon.'*

With heartfelt thanks,

Aayush Maatrishya

****

About The Author

Aayush Maatrishya

Aayush Jha, known by his pen name **Aayush Maatrishya**, is an accomplished author who has earned a reputation for captivating readers with his thought-provoking narratives. With a keen eye for storytelling and a profound passion for literature, he has penned several engaging novels and short stories. His works traverse various genres, from gripping thrillers to heartwarming dramas, showcasing his versatility as a writer.

Aayush's ability to craft compelling characters and weave intricate plots has not only won critical acclaim but also garnered him a dedicated following of avid readers.

Hailing from the vibrant city of Jamshedpur, Aayush draws inspiration from the lives and stories of the people in his community. He firmly believes in the transformative power of words and remains dedicated to inspiring and touching the hearts of readers through his literary creations.

Professional Career: Maatrishya professional journey has been intertwined with his passion for writing. He began his career as a poet, and over time, his interest turned to story writing.

Writing Style and Themes: Aayush Maatrishya is renowned for his evocative and immersive writing style. He weaves intricate narratives that delve into the complexities of human emotions and relationships. His works often explore themes of identity, true love, cultural diversity, and the human condition, resonating with readers on a profound level.

Conclusion: Aayush Maatrishya stands as a remarkable literary figure, known for his distinctive storytelling, exploration of universal themes, and his commitment to fostering cross cultural empathy through his words. His works continue to inspire readers and contribute to the world of contemporary literature.

****

Books by This Author

"Anjanne Ajnabee"

"Anjanne Ajnabee" is an emotional journey of a high school student Raahul, whose life is connected with memories, regrets and unresolved feelings. In the center of this story is Raahul's deep connection with Divya, a significant character whose presence shapes his world in a way he never imagined.

The story explores the concept of "Emotional Debt", drawing a parallel between financial and emotional obligations. Raahul, reluctant to express his true feelings to Divya, struggles with the emotional burden that has been accumulating on him for years. The story sheds light on the complexities of human relationships, missed opportunities and the importance of communication in time.

Personal and academic challenges, Raahul's journey are filled with mystery and suspense. As he faces the twists and turns and overcomes the uncertainties of life, the readers will eagerly wait for the important revelations in his story, wondering if he will finally muster the courage to reconcile with his emotional past.

"Prem: Ek Sookha Phool"

"Prem: Ek Sookha Phool" is a captivating and thought-provoking love story based on a modern Indian city. It follows the journey of two individuals, Sameer and Ananya, who create an extraordinary bond through their shared passion for literature and their romance in the midst of the city's chaos. Together, they organize literary events that take them on adventurous trips to discover the hidden gems in their cityscape.

However, their budding friendship faces a serious challenge when a misunderstanding arises, leading to a rift that strains their relationship. Hurt and confused, they drift apart, putting their once flourishing bond in danger.

Amidst the turmoil, a mysterious anonymous letter presents an element of the mystery, raising questions about the origin and consequences of their friendship. The story examines the issues of trust, communication and forgiveness as Sameer and Ananya grapple with their misconceptions.

"Prem: Ek Sookha Phool" ultimately celebrates the ability to connect through literature, the beauty found in the simple things of life and the profound bonds that emerge from unexpected conflicts. It is a story of hope, reminding the readers that friendship can be revived and love can triumph even in the face of challenges and misunderstandings.

"Meri Kya Galti Thi"

In the pages of "Meri Kya Galti Thi", we embark on a captivating and thought-provoking journey through the turbulence of life's uncertainties. It is a story of a young individual who is trapped in a bewildering world, where reality is confronted with twisted perceptions, and every step forward reveals another layer of complexity.

"Aashaadh Mein Saavan"

The poem "Aashaadh Mein Saavan" describes the beauty and love of the month of Saavan. It expresses the beauty of this season with the abundance of Saavan's melodies, rain, shining stars, and natural scenery.

The poem presents love as a unique relationship with the earth, sky, rain, and Saavan. The poem depicts the lover remembering his beloved in the manner of the season of Saavan, which is a source of new enthusiasm and happiness in life. The main purpose of this poem is to feel the connection between love and Saavan, which is still important in today's era.

****